Book Six

Violet Learns A Lesson

Copyright © 2017

World Teacher Aid All rights reserved.

Contributing Authors

Cobblestone Elementary School-Loes Cowell & Melanie McLaren

William Archer	Cole Floyd
Skylar Braithwaite	Elizabeth Gemmill
Brodie Campbell	Clara Gray
Cameron Cardy	Juliet Lund
Genevieve Carriere	Hailey Miller
Kyla Croome	Jude Osmond
Blake Cummings	Joshua Potvin
Charlie Eldridge	Makayla Quinn
Clarice Farrell	Colten Robinson
Harlow Ferguson	Bennett Ross

Contributing Authors

Cobblestone Elementary School-Loes Cowell & Melanie McLaren

Alexis Vukelich

Landon Schermerhorn

Jax Ferguson

Finley Williamson

Isabella Wolf

Savannah Skitch

Cali Sloan

Brianna Sparks

Helen Tugman

Contributing Authors

Cobblestone Elementary School-Mrs. Levac & Mrs. Hill

Addison Bingeman	Easton Rebernik
Amos Curry	Elliot Godden
Avaya Darby	Emmett Fulkerson
Benjamin Field	Grace Francis
Briar Wright	Graeson Graham
Caleb Dey	Ian Kargus
Cameron Brant	Isabelle Moffatt
Charlotte Bowman	

Contributing Authors

Cobblestone Elementary School-Mrs. Levac & Mrs. Hill

- Julia Maltby
- Juliette Paipa
- Kash Morris
- Kieran Haase
- Liam DeVries
- Maiya Martin
- Noah Belanger
- Owyn Latty
- Reghan Eddy
- Samantha Falkiner
- Scott Chesterton
- Trennen Oakes
- Vanessa McCallum

Contributing Authors

Cobblestone Elementary School-Mrs. Kingma

Mya-Sue Barrack	Addison Lee
Sarah Carter	Grayson Miller
Ruby Curry	Sydnee Sager
Aidan Darling	Will Sincerbox
Reid Francis	Cameron Sloss
Isla Haase	Jade Thibeault
Aussie Kalliokowski	Owen Watson
Finn Kargus	Emily White-Devereaux
Jack Kingsbury	Levi Wilson
	Olivia Lue-Hue

Contributing Authors

Cobblestone Elementary School-Mrs. Heidi Barnett

Ashley Cain	Luca Oakes
Shayne Chapin	Kayla Padusenko
Eden Dey	Rustin Robbins
Jackson Dicks	Ava Ross
Kaiden Gates	Desiray Schermerhorn
Bella Keyes	Canaan Sherbino
Jordan Keyes	Charlie Stevenson
Nora Kovacs	Eoin Wright
Ella Morissette	Quinn Yurkiw

Contributing Authors

Cobblestone Elementary School-Mrs. Novak's Class

Chase Benoit	Ariana Lewis
Masen Benoit	Liam Mackenzie
Paityn Blackmore	Grace McSweeney
Jake Brown	Connor Bennett
Mattis Duncan	Sam Moffatt
Andrew Graham	Jake Muskiluke
John Hart-Colling	Gabriel Ruddach
Olivia Hunt	Ally Stewart
Lukas Koenig	Rachel Tubman
Oliver Lacroix	Sema Necip

ACKNOWLEDGMENTS

A very special thank you to all those who help make Write to Give happen. Each year, the program continues to grow and have a bigger impact on Canadian and international students. This would not happen, if it were not for the hard work of the teachers who have helped implement this program.

Thank you to our teachers, Mrs. Novak, Mrs. Barnett, Mrs. Kingma, Mrs. Levac, Mrs. Hill, Mrs. Cofell, & Mrs. McLaren!

Thank you to my team of editors, designers and family who have helped with W2G 2017.

Thank you,

Amy McLaren

Violet Learns a Lesson

Copyright © 2017

World Teacher Aid All rights reserved.

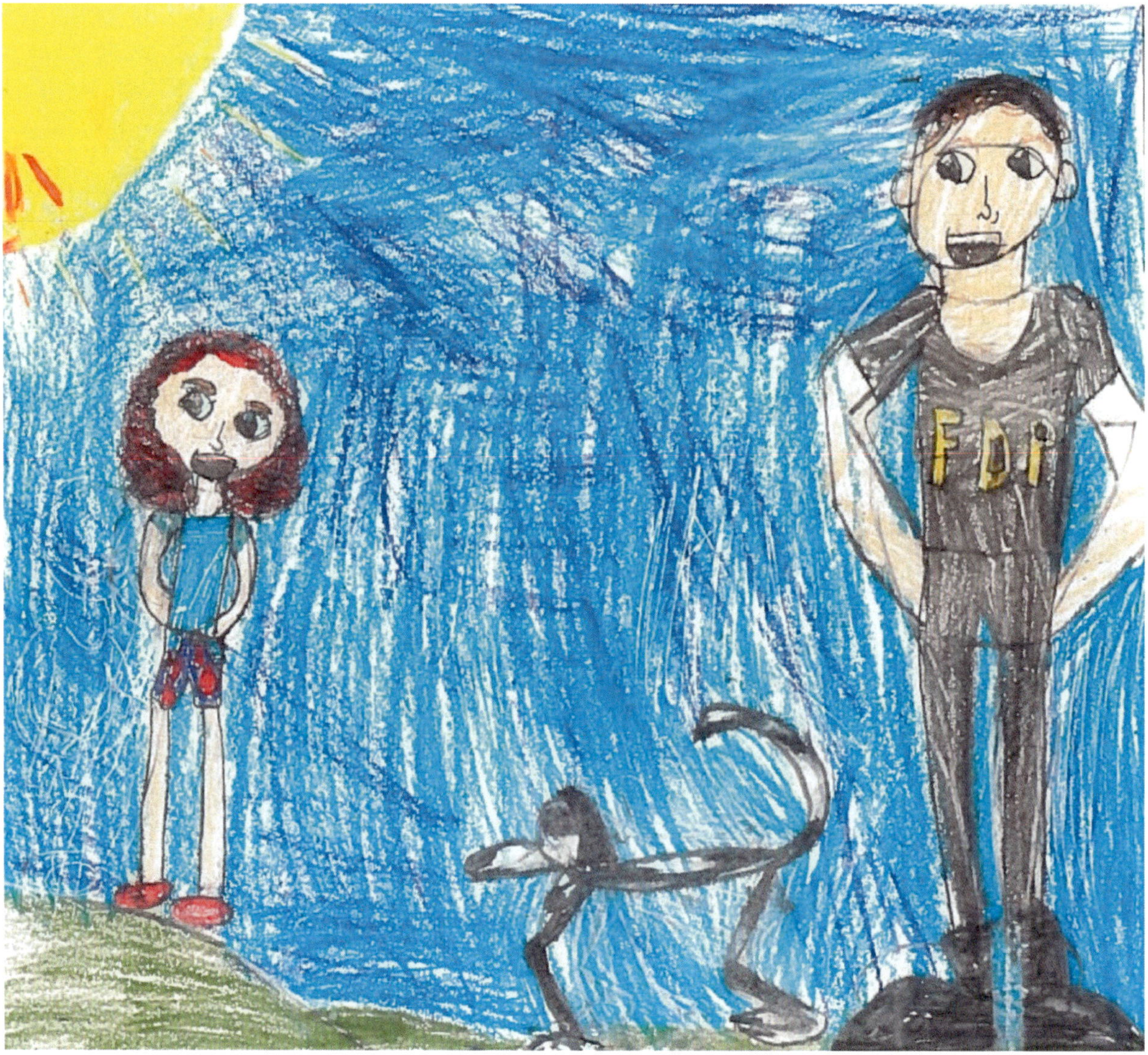

There once was a handsome firefighter named Mark. He lived in a small, red house very close to the fire station. Mark, the fire fighter, had a dog named Archie. Archie was a Dalmatian with white and black spots. He was a big, strong dog that liked to help put out fires. Archie also liked to play with a little girl named Violet.

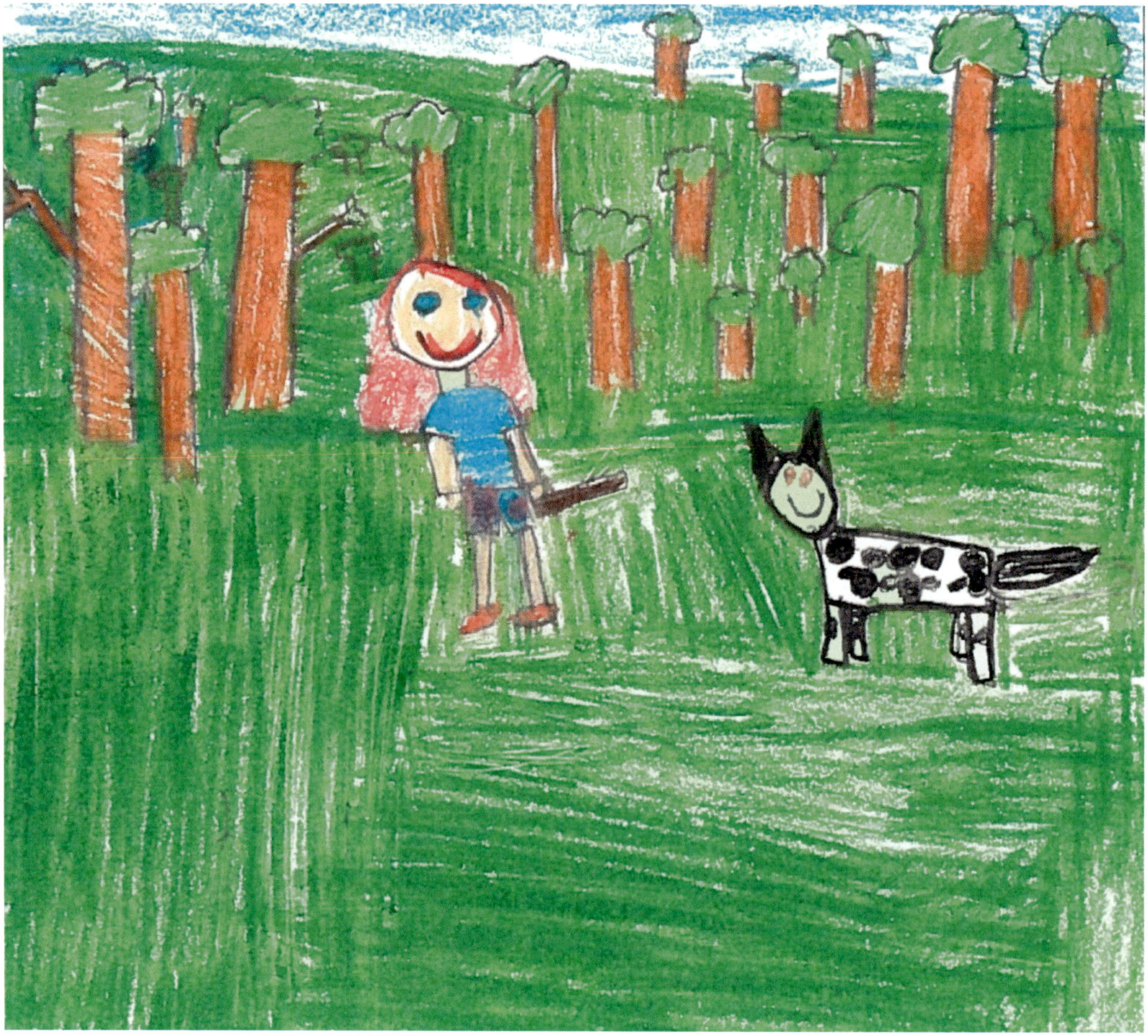

Violet lived down the street in a house as big as a castle. She was a girl with bright red curly hair, that had no brothers or sisters.

Since Violet was an only child she sometimes got lonely and always loved to play with Archie. Violet and Archie would often go for walks to the nearby park. Violet loved to bring a stick with her so she could play fetch with Archie.

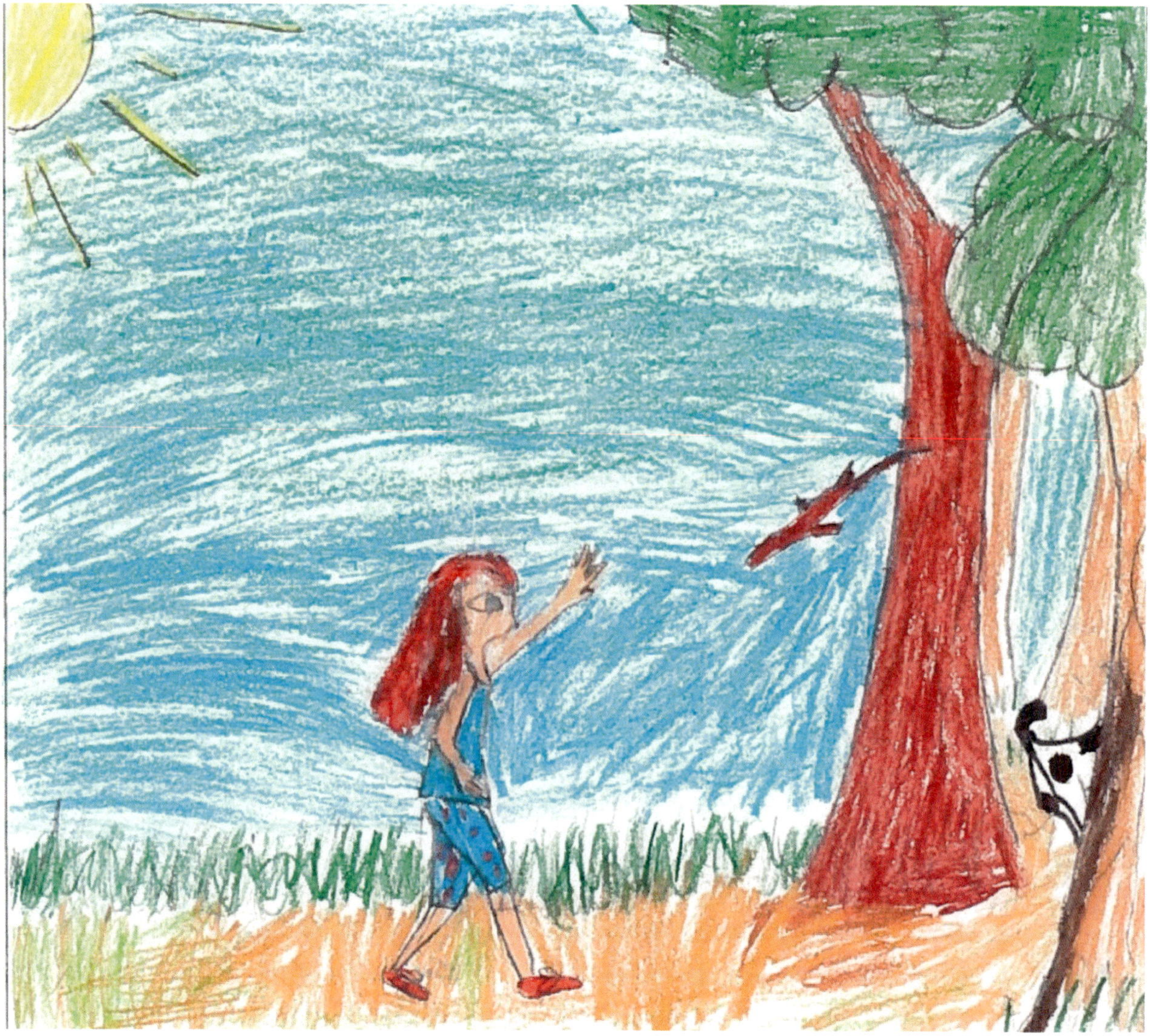

One day at the park, Violet threw the stick way into the forest. Archie ran to get the stick. Violet waited and waited for Archie to come back. She called his name, patted her legs and whistled but Archie didn't come.

She started to get nervous. It was almost time to take Archie home. Violet knew she would have to tell Mark she lost Archie. Mark might be sad or angry. Then she had an idea.

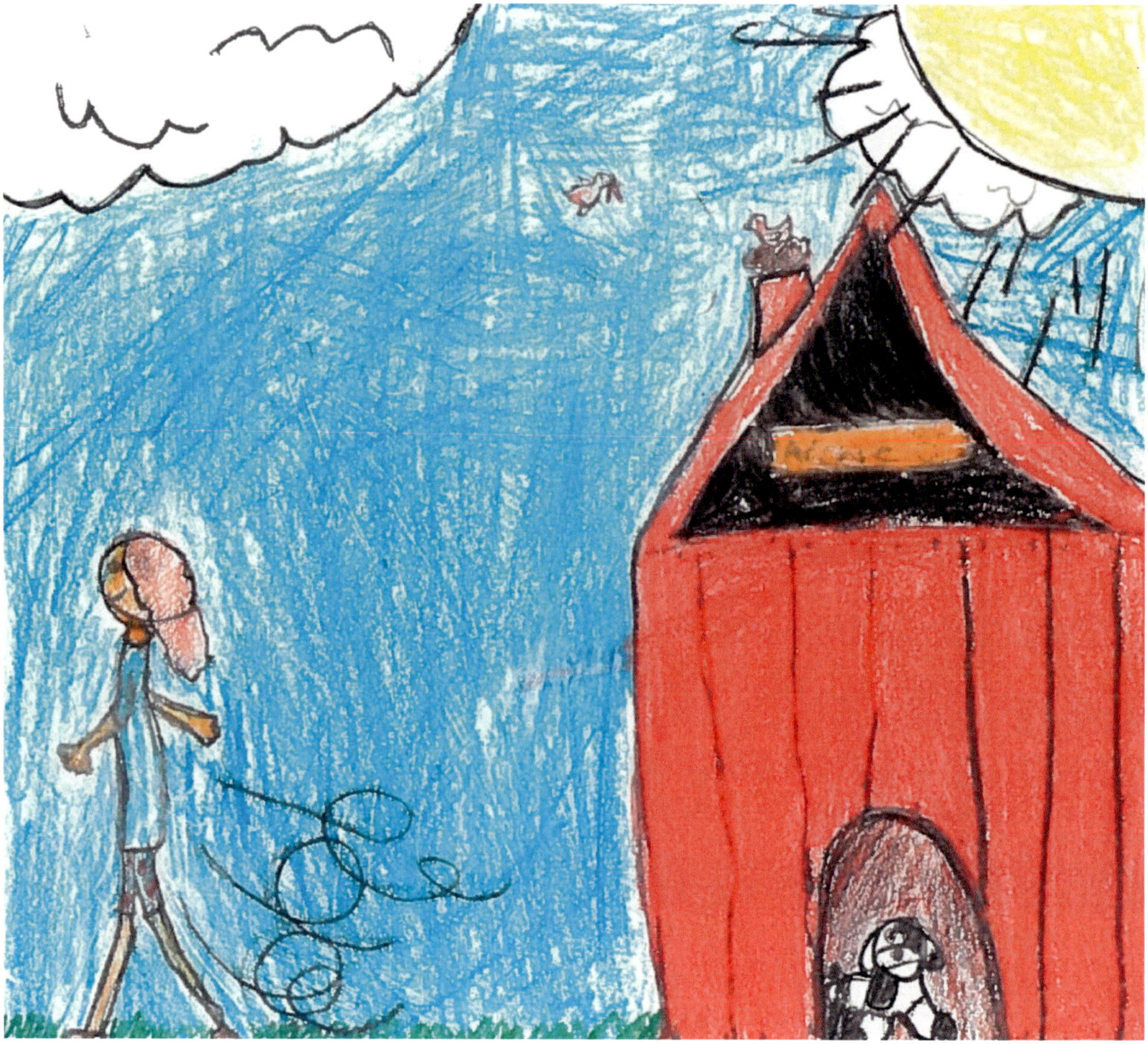

She went home and made a stuffy that looked just like Archie with black and white spots.

Then she took the fake Archie and put him in his dog house.

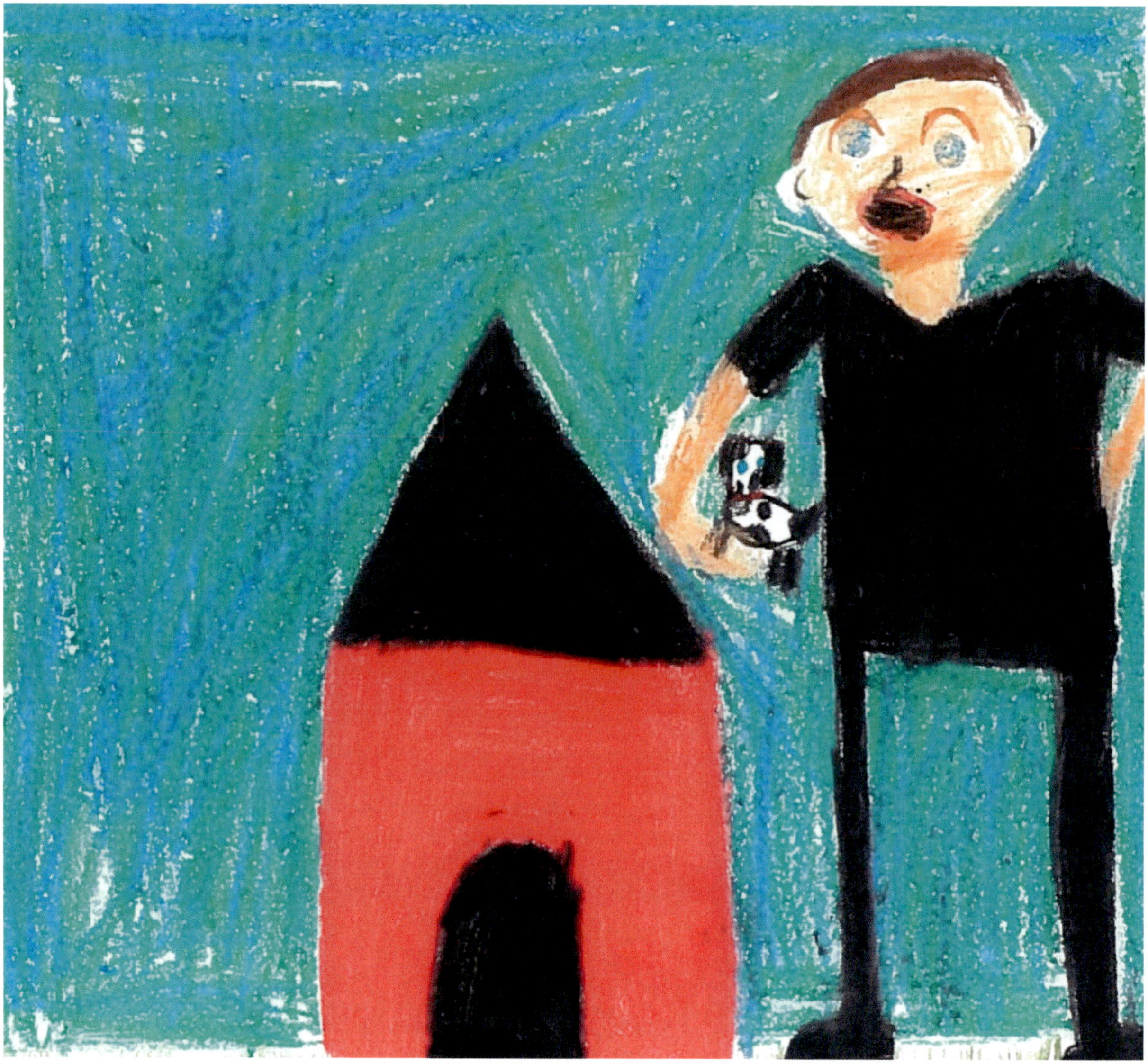

The next day, fire fighter Mark went to the fire house to pet Archie.

Mark was confused why there was a stuffy in the dog house.

So, he went to Violet's house to see if she knew where Archie was.

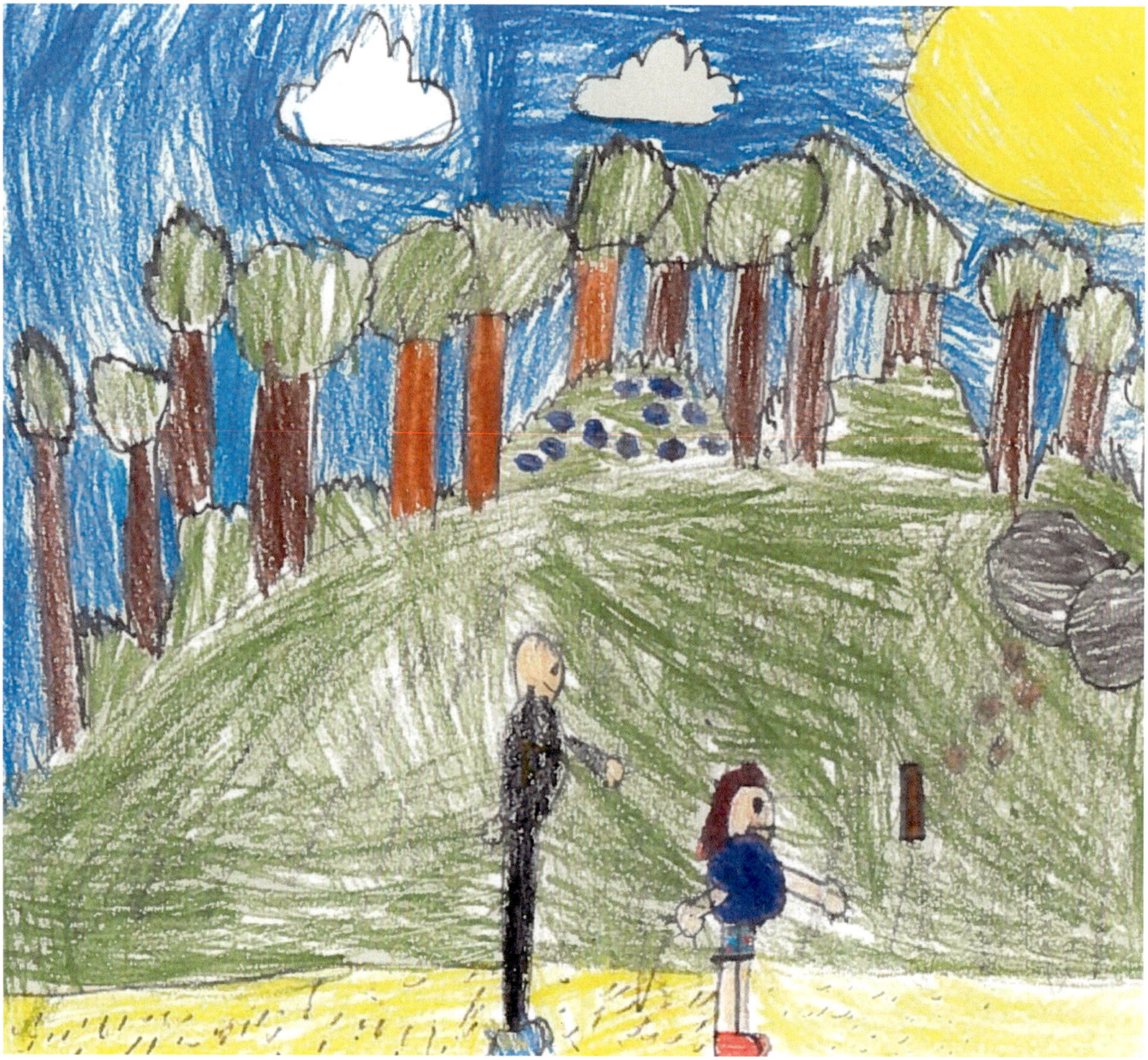

When Mark arrived at her house, Violet was frightened that she was going to get into trouble.

She decided be honest and tell Mark the truth about the dog getting lost because she didn't know what else to do.

The two of them decided to go the forest to find Archie together.

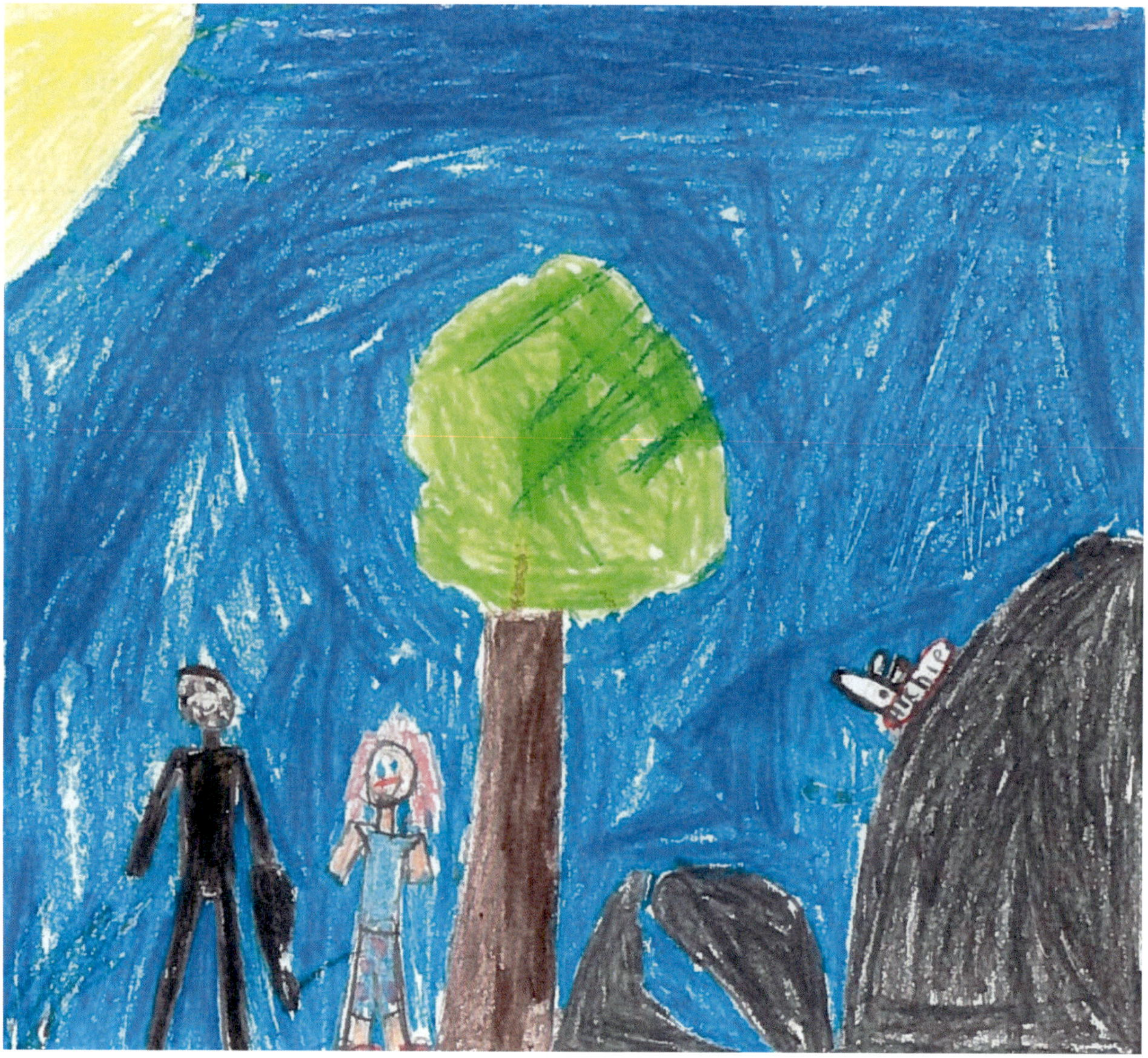

It was a sunny day so the forest wasn't too dark but it was very quiet.

Firefighter Mark whistled his special whistle that Archie knew well. Both Violet and Mark walked down the long path and suddenly Violet saw a stick that looked a lot like the stick she brought to play fetch with yesterday.

They also saw footprints that looked like Archie's. There were some rocks ahead. Mark whistled one more time and all of a sudden they heard a big bark.

Archie came running from behind the rocks and he was so happy he nearly knocked Mark over and licked his face over and over to kiss him.

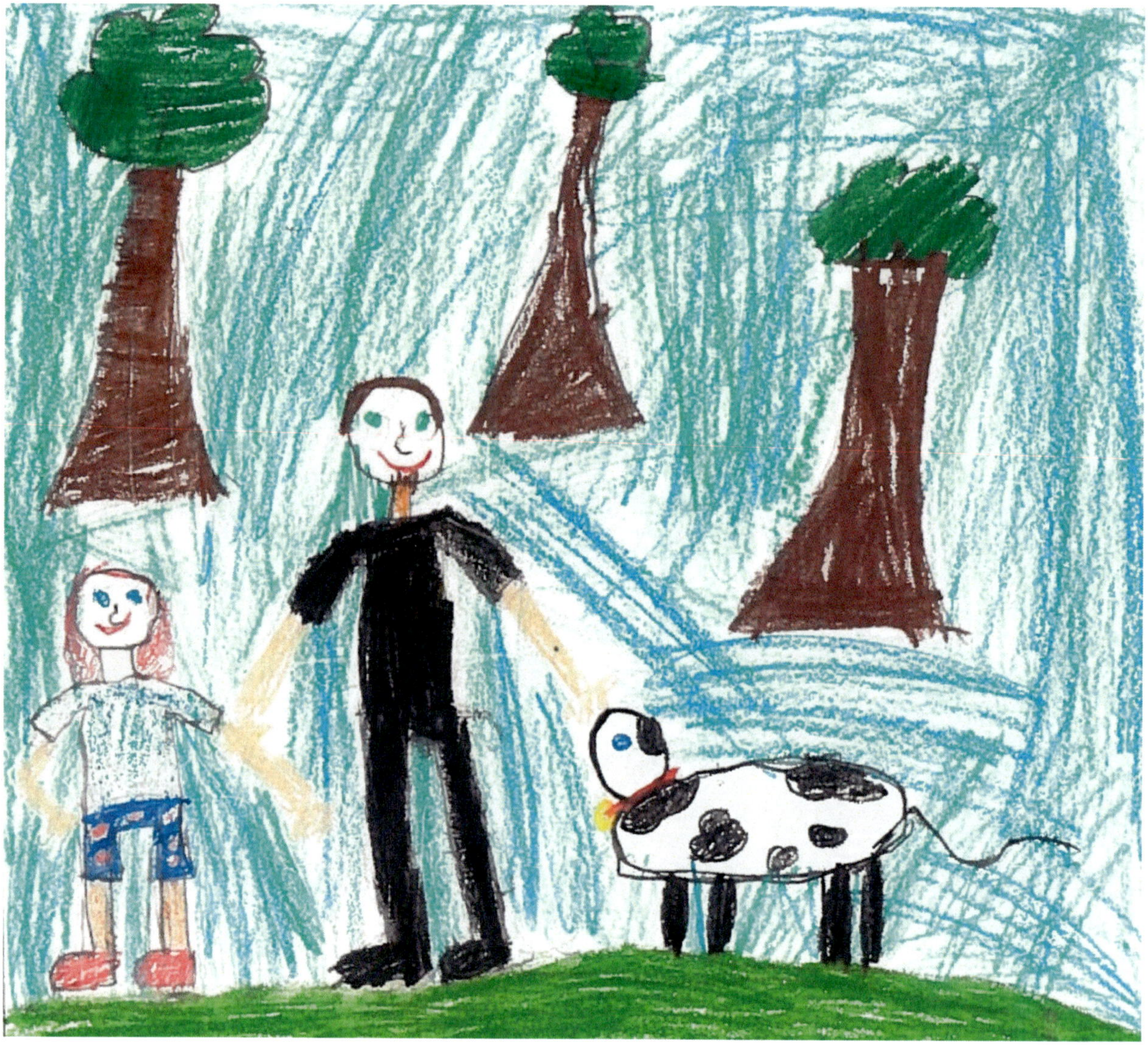

Violet learned a big lesson… she saw how much they cared for each other and knew from this day on, that she would always tell the truth no matter what!!

World Teacher Aid

World Teacher Aid is a Canadian charity committed to improving education throughout the developing world with a focus on IDP settlements (Internally Displaced Persons – communities that have been uprooted from their homes). Our current projects are within Kenya and Ghana.

As a charity we are committed to providing access to education for students within settled IDP Camps. We accomplish this vision through the renovation and/or construction of schools.

Before we begin working with a community, we ensure that they are on board with the goal. A community must be settled and show leadership before we commit to a project. We also look for commitment from the Government, ensuring that if we step in and build the school, that they will help support the ongoing expenses, such as teachers salaries, and more.

AUTOGRAPHS

AUTOGRAPHS

Made in the USA
Middletown, DE
22 April 2017